ARCHIE
THE UGLY DINOSAUR

STEGOSAURUS

2

Especially for Jack Anthony, with love

All inquiries should be addressed to:
Barron's Educational Series, Inc.
250 Wireless Boulevard
Hauppauge, New York 11788

International Standard Book No. 0-7641-0092-0

Library of Congress Catalog Card No. 96-86388

PRINTED IN BELGIUM

3

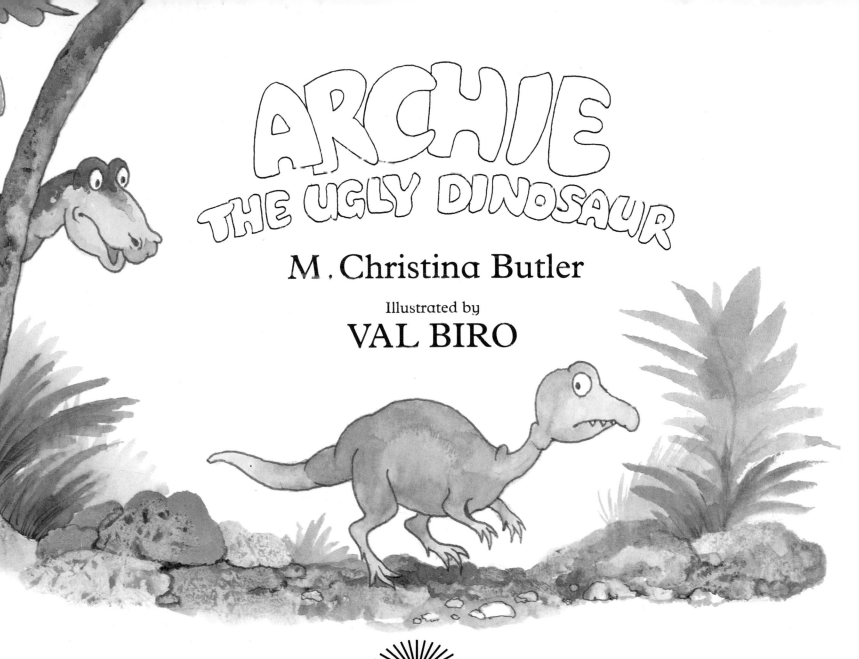

ARCHIE
THE UGLY DINOSAUR

M. Christina Butler

Illustrated by
VAL BIRO

BARRON'S

4

Not all dinosaurs were big.
Archie was very small . . .

Much smaller than his friends.

Wherever they went,
Archie's legs were so small,

he was always left behind.

8

And whatever they did,

Archie was usually in the way.

He tried everything,

but nothing seemed to make him bigger.

Then Archie woke up one morning and FELT he was growing at last.
But when he looked down at himself, he was covered all over in little spikes!

Everyone laughed when they saw him.

They laughed so much,

that Archie ran away, deep into the forest.

16

When Archie had gone,
the big dinosaurs
began blaming
each other.
"You shouldn't have
laughed at him,"
said Triceratops.

"Well you laughed first,"
cried Stegosaurus.
Diplodocus was
thoughtful.
"The forest is
a dangerous place
for a small dinosaur,"
she said.
"We'd better find
him before the
big Rexes do."

17

They began to look at once.

They searched by day,

and they searched . . .

by night.

22

They came to the
mountains where the
big Rexes lived.
"I don't like it here,"
Triceratops whispered.

So they stopped and called out,

23

"ARCHIE ... ARE YOU THERE?"

Suddenly the big Rexes
came out with a
ROAR!

25

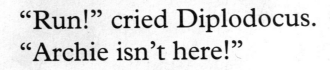

"Run!" cried Diplodocus.
"Archie isn't here!"

26

"Yes I am!" answered a voice.

"I'm up here!"

Archie had grown into a BIRD!
A beautiful ARCHAEOPTERYX.

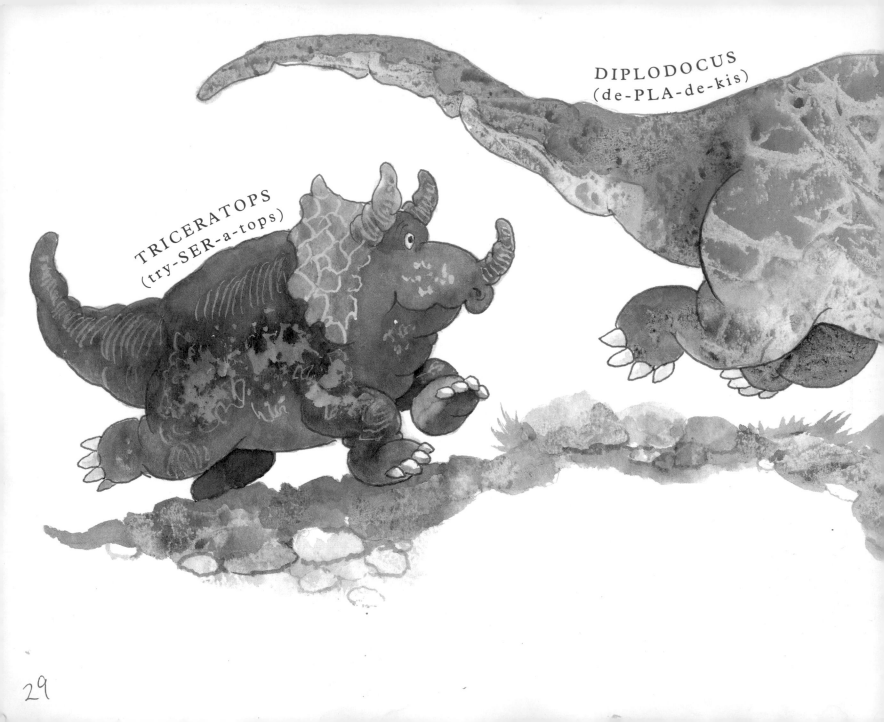

ARCHAEOPTERYX
(ar-kee-AP-te-rix)

STEGOSAURUS
(STEG-oh-SAW-rus)